I Din Do Nuttin

ALSO BY JOHN AGARD

Say it Again, Granny

A Red Fox Book
Published by Random House Children's Books
20 Vauxhall Bridge Road, London SW1V 2SA

First published by
The Bodley Head Children's Books 1983
Red Fox edition 1993
Poems © John Agard 1983
Illustrations © Susanna Gretz 1983

John Agard and Susanna Gretz have
asserted their rights to be identified as the
author and illustrator of this work

Printed and bound in Great Britain by
Cox & Wyman Ltd, Reading, Berkshire

RANDOM HOUSE UK Limited Reg. No. 954009
ISBN 0 09 918451 6

I Din Do Nuttin

and other poems by
John Agard

Illustrated by
Susanna Gretz

RED FOX

I DIN DO NUTTIN

I din do nuttin
I din do nuttin
I din do nuttin
All I did
was throw Granny pin
in the rubbish bin.

I din do nuttin
I din do nuttin
I din do nuttin
All I did
was mix paint in
Mammy biscuit tin.

I din do nuttin
I din do nuttin.

HAPPY BIRTHDAY, DILROY!

My name is Dilroy.
I'm a little black boy
and I'm eight today.

My birthday cards say
it's great to be eight
and they sure right
coz I got a pair of skates
I want for a long long time.

My birthday cards say,
Happy Birthday, Dilroy!
But, Mummy, tell me why
they don't put a little boy
that looks a bit like me.
Why the boy on the card so white?

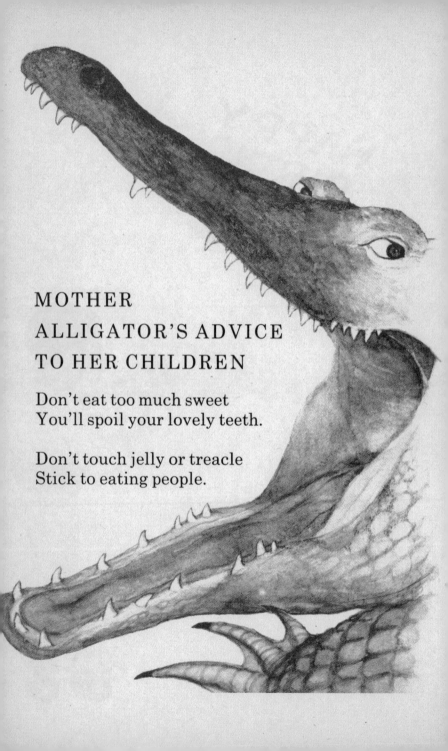

MOTHER ALLIGATOR'S ADVICE TO HER CHILDREN

Don't eat too much sweet
You'll spoil your lovely teeth.

Don't touch jelly or treacle
Stick to eating people.

A BABY BROTHER

Today
I told Mummy
I have a baby
in my tummy.

She laughed
But it's true
Really, really.

At school you see
Miss said a baby
comes from a seed,

So today
I swallowed one.
I really need
a baby brother.

SNOW-CONE

Snow-cone nice
Snow-cone sweet
Snow-cone is crush ice
and good for the heat.

When sun really hot
and I thirsty a lot,
Me alone,
Yes me alone,
could eat ten snow-cone.

If you think is lie I tell
wait till you hear the snow-cone bell,
wait till you hear the snow-cone bell.

strawberry peach
raspberry coffee
blueberry Blackberry
cherry Pineapple
Lemon
Banana tangerine
Pear chocolate
Lime
Peppermint
Orange

STOP TROUBLING
THAT PHONE

Telephone,
telephone,
you're so alone

Like a king
with no throne

Like a dog
with no bone.

Telephone,
telephone,
you look so bored.

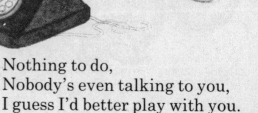

Nothing to do,
Nobody's even talking to you,
I guess I'd better play with you.

ASK MUMMY ASK DADDY

When I ask Daddy
Daddy says ask Mummy

When I ask Mummy
Mummy says ask Daddy.
I don't know where to go.

Better ask my teddy
he never says no.

FISHING

Fishing all day long
and can't catch a thing.

What's wrong? What's wrong?
I ask the little worm
at the end of my hook.

The worm give me one look
and start to sing this song:

'Fish like to slip
in deep rain
Not take a dip
in frying pan.'

SAY CHEESE

Take a picture of me
and let my Mummy see.

Take a picture of me
Please, please, please!

But I don't wanna say cheese
and smile.

I wanna say ice-cream
and SCREAM!

HIGH HEELS

I wonder
how it feels
to wear high heels
like my big sister?

Coz I'm smaller
I have to wait
longer
for high heels
to make me taller.

I wonder
how it feels
to wear high heels
and have corns
on your toes
and a blister?

I suppose
I'd better
ask my big sister.

THREE-HOLE

Three-hole
is the name
of a marble game
we got in Guyana.

Is fun to play
and not hard.
Just dig three lil holes
in you yard
or the sand
by you gate.
Then aim straight

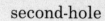

second-hole

for first-hole

third-hole.

If you lucky
and you marble
go in all the holes
one two three

Then is you chance
to knock you friend marble.
Send it flying for a dance.
When marble burst then fun start.

SUGARCANE

When I take
a piece of sugarcane
and put it to me mouth
I does suck and suck
till all the juice come out.

I don't care
if is sun or rain
I does suck and suck
till all the juice come out.

But when I doing homewuk
and same time playing bout
Granny does tell me,
'How you can work properly
and play at the same time?
You brain can't settle.
I always telling you
you can't suck cane and whistle,
you can't suck cane and whistle!'

NEW SHOES

Buying new shoes
takes so long.
When the colour is right
the size is wrong.

The lady asks
How does it fit?
I say to Mum
Pinches a bit.

But that's not true
It's just because
I don't want the brown
I prefer the blue.

The lady goes inside
brings another size
this time the blue.
Not too big. Not too tight.

As you guessed
Just right, just right.
Mum says, 'The blue will do.'
And I agree. Don't you?

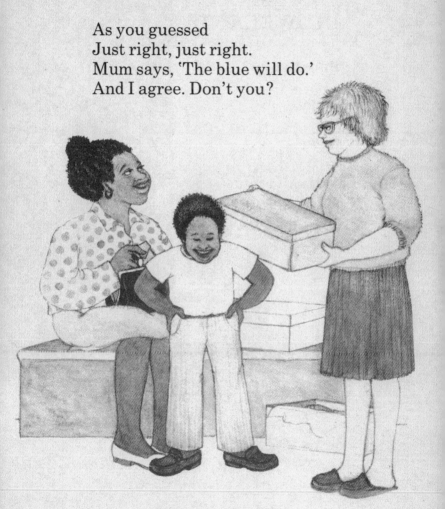

IF I COULD ONLY TAKE HOME A SNOWFLAKE

Snowflakes
like tiny
insects
drifting
down.

Without a hum
they come,
Without a hum
they go.

Snowflakes
like tiny
insects
drifting
down.

If only
I could take
one
home with me
to show
my friends
in the sun,
just for fun,
just for fun.

DUCK-BELLY BIKE

Teacher B
got a duck-belly
bike

And everybody like
Teacher B
duck-belly
bike.

It get the name
because the frame
so round
and bulging out

But one boy name Mack
so good at telling lie
he say is because
the bike does go
quack quack.

MY TELLY

My telly
eats people
especially
on the news.

Little people
with no shoes
Little people
with no food
Little people
crying
Little people
dying.

My telly
eats people.
If you don't
believe me
look inside
the belly
of my telly.

MY RABBIT

My rabbit
has funny habits.

When I say sit
he sits.

When he hears me call
he wags
his tail a bit.

When I throw a ball
he grabs it.

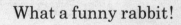

What a funny rabbit!

One day in the park
I swore I heard him bark.

MICKY ALWAYS

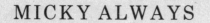

Bambalitty-Bambam,
Bambalitty-Bambam,
Everybody scram, scram.

Micky hit the ball so hard
it gone right out the yard
and break the lady window-pane.
He Micky don't hear, just don't hear.

SORRY, MUM!

I didn't mean to scratch the match.
I didn't mean to make the fire catch.
I didn't mean to burn the house down.
I was only playing fireman!

Sorry, mum!
Sorry, mum!
Sorry, mum!

What's the good
of that?

A whack
on your bum
won't bring
the house back.

LOLLIPOP LADY

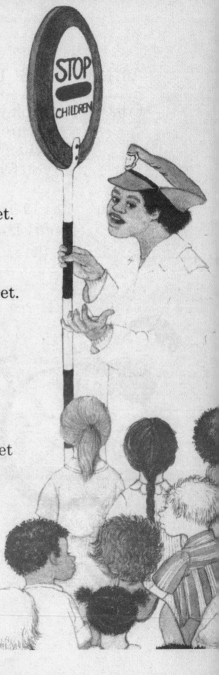

Lollipop lady,
lollipop lady,
wave your magic stick
and make the traffic
stop a while
so we can cross the street.

Trucks and cars
rushing past
have no time for little feet.
They hate to wait
especially when late
but we'll be late too
except for you.

So lollipop lady,
lollipop lady,
in the middle of the street
wave your magic stick
and make the traffic
give way to little feet.

ALL FOOLS' DAY

First voice : Look you bicycle wheel
                turning round!
                When you look down
                you feel like a clown.

Chorus : *Yay, Yay,*
             Today is All Fools' Day!

Second Voice : Look you drop a penny
pon the ground!
When you think you lucky
and look down,
Not a thing like money
pon the ground.

Chorus : *Yay, Yay,*
Today is All Fools' Day!

Third Voice : Look you shoelace loose out!
When you hear the shout
and look down at you shoe
It ain't true, it ain't true.

Chorus : *Yay, Yay,*
Today is All Fools' Day!

Fourth Voice : Look you mother calling you!
Look you mother calling you!
Is true, is true, is true!

First Voice : Well let she call till she blue,
            I ain't going nowhay.
            You ain't ketching me this time
            Today is All Fools' Day.

Mother's Voice : Kenrick! Kenrick! Kenrrriicckk!
               See how long I calling this boy
               and he playing he ain't hear.
               When he come I gon cut he tail!

HI, COCONUT

Coconut tree
so tall and high
when I look up at yuh
I got to wink up me eye.

Coconut tree
yuh coconut big
like football in the sky.
Drop down one fo me nuh.

If only I could reach yuh
if only I could reach yuh
is sweet water and jelly
straight to me belly.

But right now coconut
yuh deh up so high
I can't reach yuh
I could only tell yuh,

                    Hi,

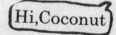

Hi, Coconut

CAT IN THE DARK

Look at that!
Look at that!

But when you look
there's no cat.

Without a purr
just a flash of fur
and gone
like a ghost.

The most
you see
are two tiny
green traffic lights
staring at the night.

Join the RED FOX Reader's Club

The Red Fox Readers' Club is for readers of all ages. All you have to do is ask your local bookseller or librarian for a Red Fox Reader's Club card. As an official Red Fox Reader you will qualify for your own Red Fox Reader's Clubpack – full of exciting surprises! If you have any difficulty obtaining a Red Fox Readers' Club card please write to: Random House Children's Books Marketing Department, 20 Vauxhall Bridge Road, London SW1V 2SA.

Other great reads from **Red Fox**

Further Red Fox titles that you might enjoy reading are listed on the following pages. They are available in bookshops or they can be ordered directly from us.

If you would like to order books, please send this form and the money due to:

ARROW BOOKS, BOOKSERVICE BY POST, PO BOX 29, DOUGLAS, ISLE OF MAN, BRITISH ISLES. Please enclose a cheque or postal order made out to Arrow Books Ltd for the amount due, plus 75p per book for postage and packing to a maximum of £7.50, both for orders within the UK. For customers outside the UK, please allow £1.00 per book.

NAME_____

ADDRESS_____

_____

Please print clearly.

Whilst every effort is made to keep prices low, it is sometimes necessary to increase cover prices at short notice. If you are ordering books by post, to save delay it is advisable to phone to confirm the correct price. The number to ring is THE SALES DEPARTMENT 071 (if outside London) 973 9700.

Other great reads from **Red Fox**

Discover the Red Fox poetry collections

CADBURY'S NINTH BOOK OF CHILDREN'S POETRY

Poems by children aged 4–16.

ISBN 0 09 983450 2   £4.99

THE COMPLETE SCHOOL VERSE
ed. Jennifer Curry

Two books in one all about school.

ISBN 0 09 991790 4   £2.99

MY NAME, MY POEM ed. Jennifer Curry

Find *your* name in this book.

ISBN 0 09 948030 1   £1.95

MONSTROSITIES Charles Fuge

Grim, gruesome poems about monsters.

ISBN 0 09 967330 4   £3.50

LOVE SHOUTS AND WHISPERS Vernon Scannell

Read about all sorts of love in this book.

ISBN 0 09 973950 X   £2.99

CATERPILLAR STEW Gavin Ewart

A collection describing all sorts of unusual animals.

ISBN 0 09 967280 4   £2.50

HYSTERICALLY HISTORICAL Gordon Snell and Wendy Shea

Madcap rhymes from olden times

ISBN 0 09 972160 0   £2.99